Mama
Mama

Mama, Mama,
Nuzzle, hug,
I'm your little
Golden cub.

Mama, Mama,
Soft as silk,
Give me warmth
And give me milk.

Mama, Mama,
Make me clean,
Every day
The same routine!

Mama, Mama,
Play with me,
Carry me
So I can see.

Mama, Mama,
Hold me tight,
We sleep a cozy
Sleep tonight.

Mama, Mama,
Show the way,
I am learning
Every day.

Mama, Mama,
You are fine,
You are clever,
You are mine.